D0884303

The Last Lemon

Copyright © Lisa Swerling and Ralph Lazar 2002
Published under exclusive licence by MQ Publications Ltd
The moral rights of the authors have been asserted

Sixth Avenue Books™ are published by:
AOL Time Warner Book Group
1271 Ave. of the Americas
New York, NY 10020

Visit our Web site at www.twbookmark.com

An AOL Time Warner Company

Printed in China
First printing: 10 9 8 7 6 5 4 3 2 1

ISBN: 1-931722-15-3

The Last Lemon

A tale of enlightenment

BY LISA SWERLING & RALPH LAZAR

Sixth Avenue Books™

An AOL Time Warner Company

The Guardian of the
lemon tree
guarded the
lemon tree.

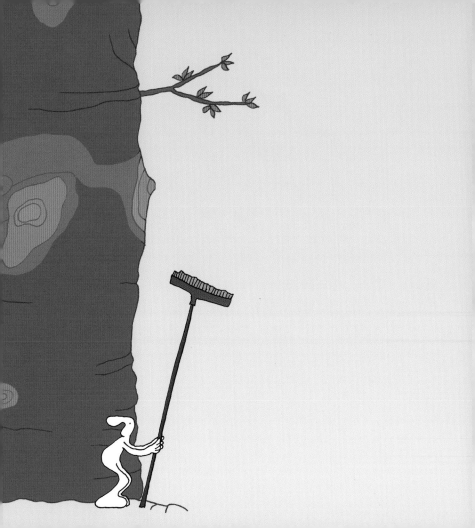

He did a very good job.

It wasn't easy, because a lot of people wanted lemons.

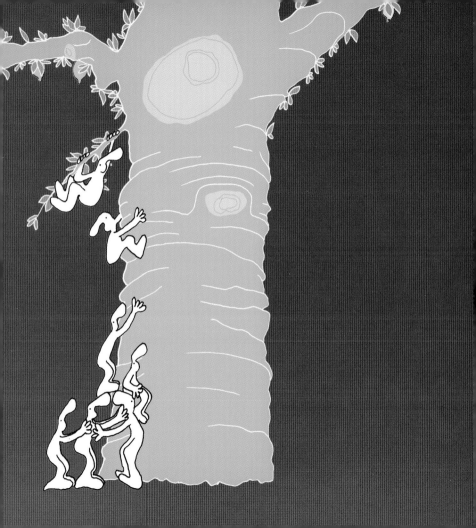

Luckily his skills as a guardian were unsurpassed.

Day
and
night he kept watch.

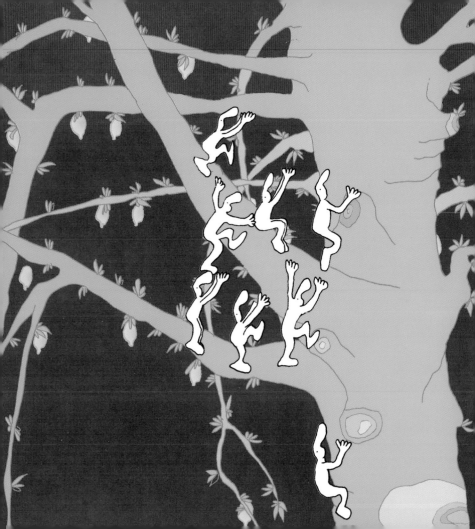

As
the Guardian's reputation
spread, so his job grew
more difficult.
It seemed that everyone
wanted lemons.

One night
he was so tired
warding off thieves,
he fell
asleep.

When the Guardian awoke...

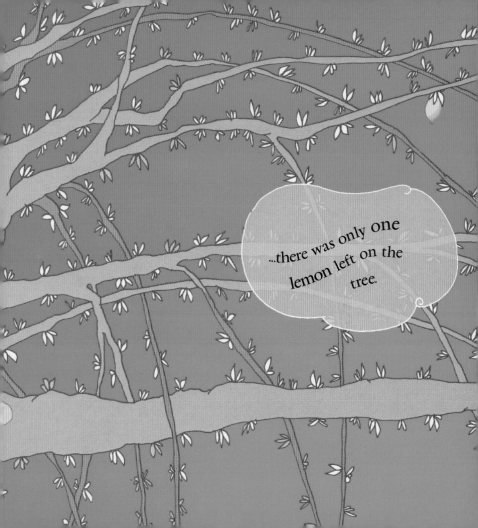

...there was only one lemon left on the tree.

The last lemon.

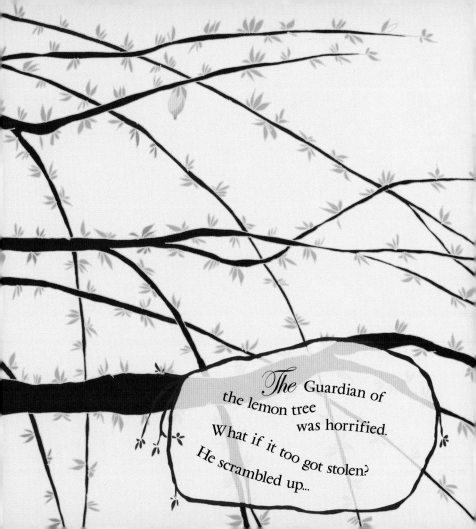

The Guardian of the lemon tree was horrified. What if it too got stolen? He scrambled up...

...and rescued
the last lemon.

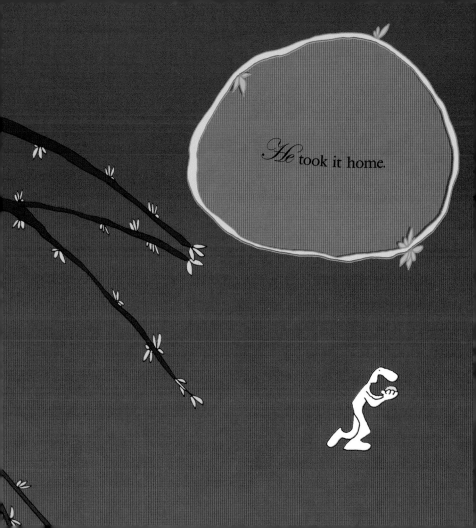

He took it home.

There he planted
the last lemon
in a pot.

His vigil began.

Soon

some shoots

appeared.

The Guardian was still
worried about the
seedling's survival.

It was a jungle
out there.

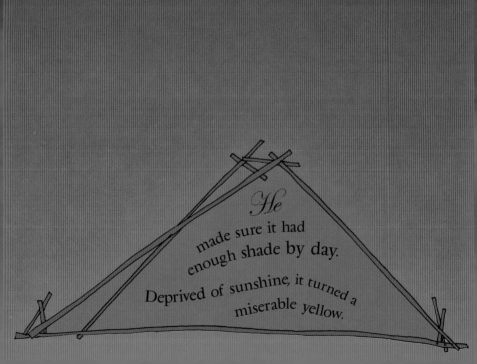

He
made sure it had
enough shade by day.
Deprived of sunshine, it turned a
miserable yellow.

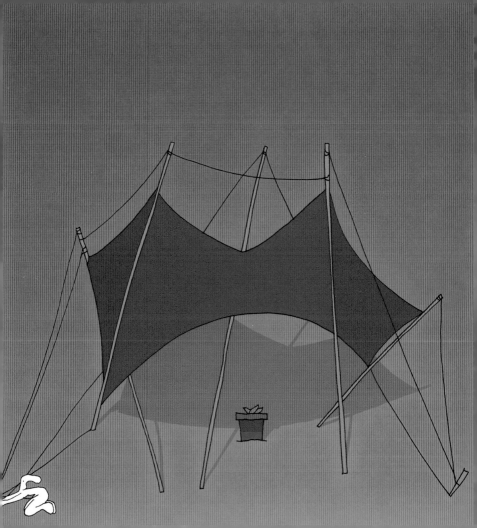

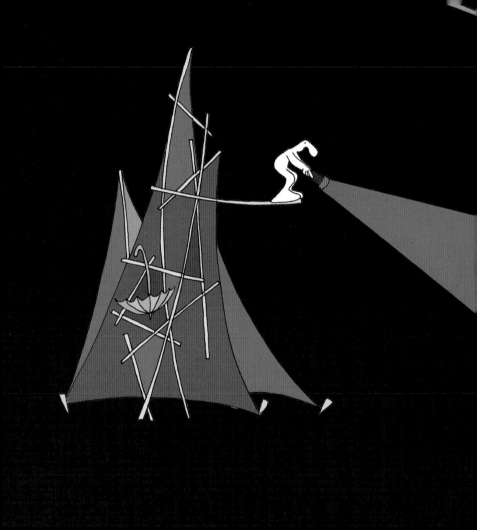

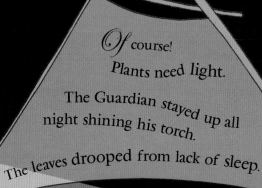

Of course!

Plants need light.

The Guardian stayed up all night shining his torch.

The leaves drooped from lack of sleep.

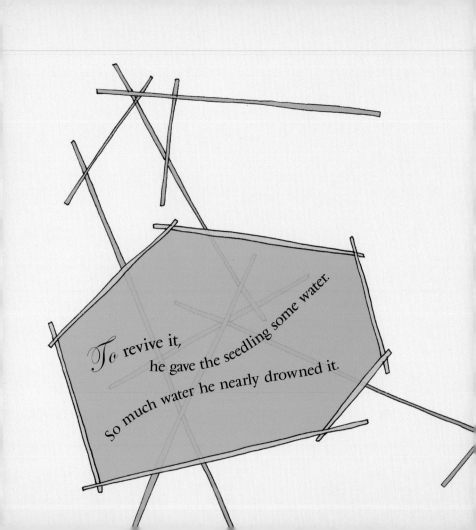

To revive it,
          he gave the seedling some water.
So much water he nearly drowned it.

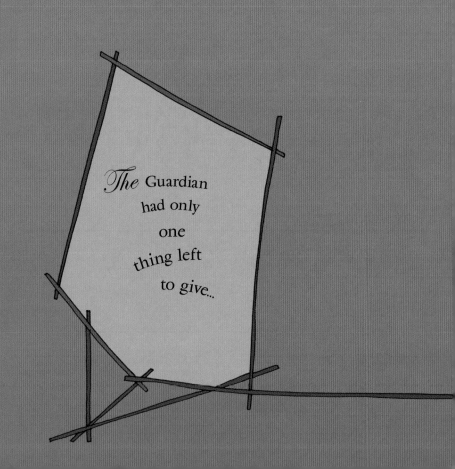

The Guardian
had only
one
thing left
to give...

...his love.

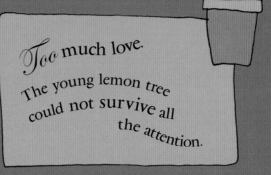

Too much love.

The young lemon tree
could not survive all
the attention.

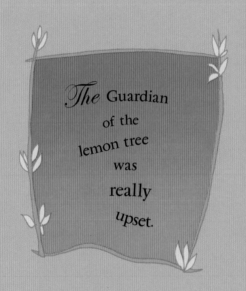

The Guardian
of the
lemon tree
was
really
upset.

He gathered

his belongings...

...and headed off
across the
open plain.

The Guardian turned for a final look
at the place he was leaving.

Far in the distance
                  he saw a tree.

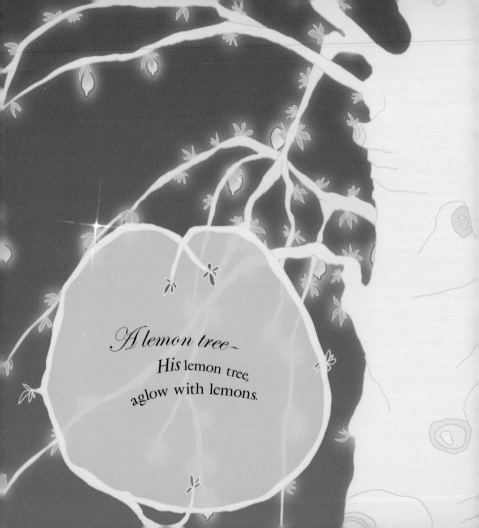

A lemon tree—
His lemon tree,
aglow with lemons.

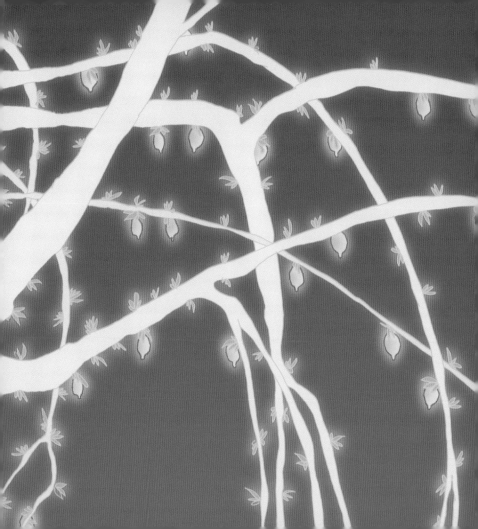

As there had been no Guardian standing watch, no-one had troubled to steal them.

ABOUT THE AUTHORS

Ralph Lazar, Lisa Swerling and their daughter
Bea are currently based in the UK. They have
recently applied for visas to Harold's Planet,
and are expected to move there as soon as
the paperwork has been processed.

This book is for Rob and Sue